ALSO BY ED SHANKMAN AND DAVE O'NEILL

The Boston Balloonies

The Cods of Cape Cod *(Spring 2009)*

ALSO BY ED SHANKMAN, WITH DAVE FRANK

I Went to the Party in Kalamazoo *(2001)*

For more information about children's books by Shankman & O'Neill, visit www.shankmanoneill.com.

I Met a Moose in Maine One Day

ISBN 978-1-933212-77-7

Designed by John Barnett/4 Eyes Design

Printed in Korea

Published by Commonwealth Editions, an imprint of Applewood Books, Inc.
Carlisle, Massachusetts 01741
Visit us on the web at www.commonwealtheditions.com.

10 9

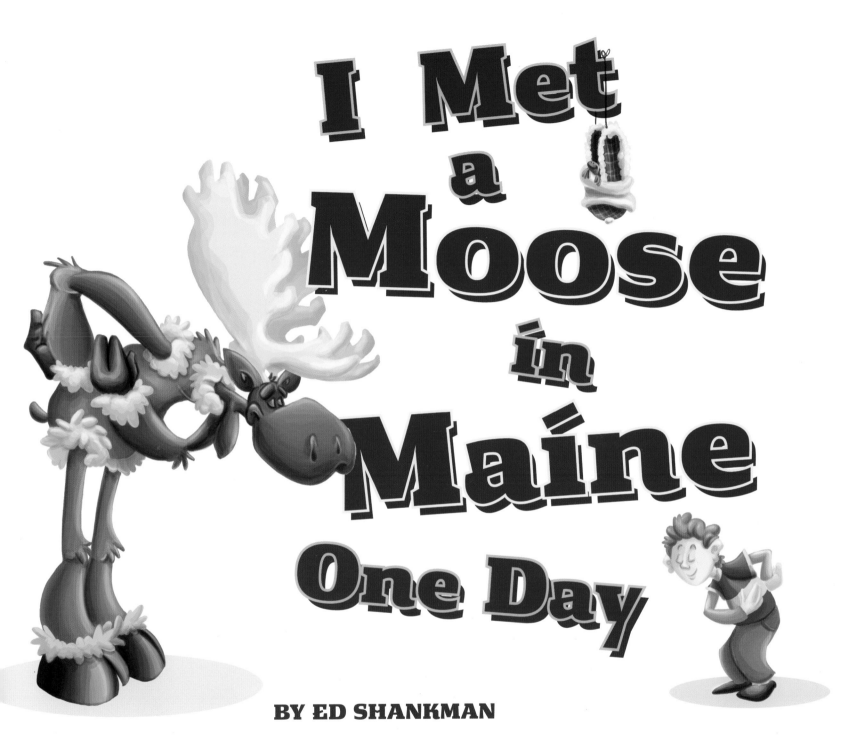

I Met a Moose in Maine One Day

BY ED SHANKMAN

ILLUSTRATED BY DAVE O'NEILL

Commonwealth Editions

Carlisle, Massachusetts

I met a moose
In Maine one day.
Just how it happened,
I can't say.

I brushed my teeth.
I combed my hair.
And all at once
The moose was there.

In Maine, as you know,
The moose come and go.
They relax in the streams.
They make tracks in the snow.

They live in the woods
With the bear and the hare.
And whatever they're doing,.
They do it out there.

That is why, in this case,
Something seemed out of place,
To be here with a moose
In my house, face to face.

The moose was so big,
So wide and so tall,
I was not sure at all
He could squeeze through the hall.

He tried to be small,
And he made sure to crawl,
But those antlers of his
Still left marks on the wall!

I don't mean to suggest
That the beast was a pest.
In fact, I felt blessed
Just to have such a guest.

'Cause by any measure
This moose was a treasure.
His smile was charming,
His manners, a pleasure.

We shared a few laughs.
We talked quite a lot.
And he told me some things
That I never forgot.

Then we played hide and seek,
But it was no use.
It seems this is not
The best game for a moose.

And then, after that,
We decided to race,
But a moose, when he runs,
Needs a great deal of space.

He smashed every bottle
And jar in the place,
And the napkins I had
Were too small for his face.

So I took him outside,
And we walked for a while,
Until we reached town,
Which is more than a mile.

If you want to meet friends
And you need an excuse,
I suggest that you walk
Into town with a moose.

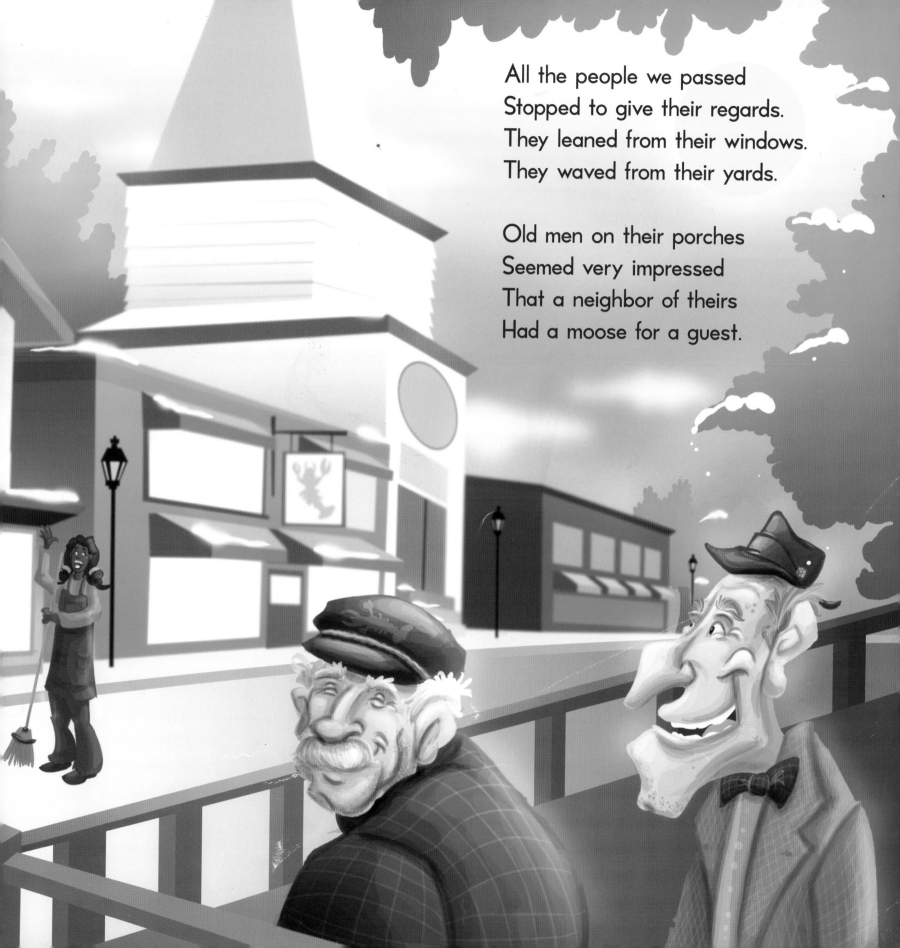

All the people we passed
Stopped to give their regards.
They leaned from their windows.
They waved from their yards.

Old men on their porches
Seemed very impressed
That a neighbor of theirs
Had a moose for a guest.

I bought a few things
That a moose never buys
Because everyone knows
A moose loves a surprise!

I bought him some fudge,

And a lumberjack's hat,

And some great maple syrup,
And, boy, he liked that.

'Cause you know maple syrup's the best thing by far
That anyone's ever put into a jar.

And the hat, I must say,
Was precisely his size,
In a blue that I thought
Really brought out his eyes!

At night, we went dancing.
We really let loose.

And there's nothing quite like
Letting loose with a moose.

We did a few things
That a moose rarely does,
And if that sounds exciting,
Believe me, it was!

But this was just one
Little village in Maine.
There were many to see
So we hopped on a plane.

From Auburn to Belfast,
From Friendship to Lee,
That moose and I saw
Every sight we could see.

We walked every walk
And we viewed every view,
And the moose I met took me
To Wallagrass too!

In Camden a lot of us
Got on a yacht,
And we docked before dark
In a beautiful spot.

We saw fish having fun.
We watched seals eating meals.
We met lobsters and otters
And eagles and eels.

In Bangor we climbed
On a raft made of logs,
And we floated downriver
With beavers and frogs.

We hopped and we jumped,

And we rocked and we rolled,

As we rushed through the rapids
Like loggers of old.

We stopped off in Portland
One beautiful day
To eat a fine lunch
In an outdoor café.

We ordered the salmon
With blueberry juice.
And there's no better juice
You can drink with a moose.

We left room for dessert
'Cause we heard that they make
The world's best selection
Of chocolate Moose cake!

When we'd had all our fun,
And our travel was done,
We stopped by the roadside
And stood in the sun.

I think we were somewhere
Near Smithfield or Rome,
When the moose I met said
It was time to go home.

He gave me a wink
And I gave him a smile.
We hugged and we said
Our goodbyes for a while.

Then he went on his way,
But he made sure to say,
That he knew he would come back
And see me some day.

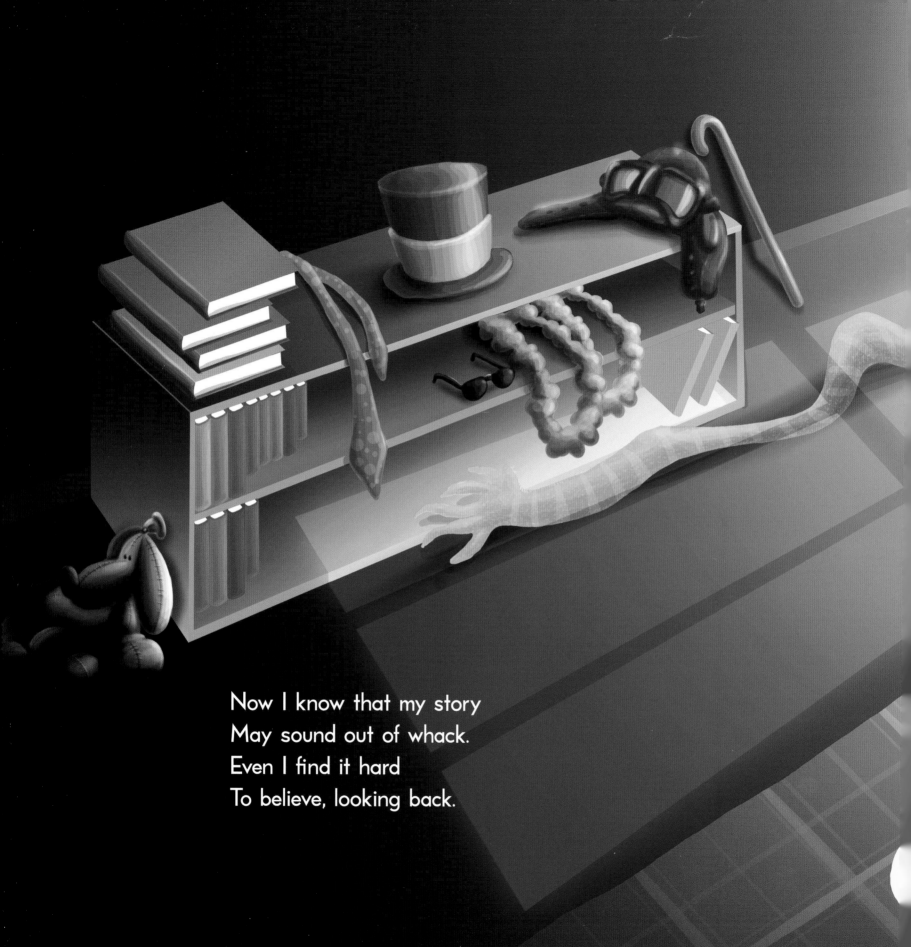

Now I know that my story
May sound out of whack.
Even I find it hard
To believe, looking back.

But it wasn't a dream
And it wasn't pretend.
I did meet a moose,
And that moose is my friend.